This book belongs to

_____

WE HAD FUN in Quarantine

LACEY J. HEINZ

ILLUSTRATED BY
HANNAH MOORE

Archway Publishing books may be ordered through booksellers or by contacting:

Archway Publishing
1663 Liberty Drive
Bloomington, IN 47403
www.archwaypublishing.com
1 (888) 242-5904

Interior Image Credit: Hannah Moore

ISBN: 978-1-4808-9471-6 (sc)
ISBN: 978-1-4808-9472-3 (hc)
ISBN: 978-1-4808-9470-9 (e)

Print information available on the last page.

Archway Publishing rev. date: 11/09/2020

This book is dedicated to my children.

Thank you for making this time in
quarantine truly memorable.

We had fun in quarantine.

We washed hands.

We rode bikes.

And we played trains
in quarantine.

We built forts.

We saw cars.

And we played trains
in quarantine.

We wore masks.

We found bears.

And we played trains in quarantine.

We watched shows.

We baked treats.

And we played trains in quarantine.

We sang songs.

We homeschooled.

And we played trains in quarantine.

We FaceTimed.

We sent mail.

And we played
trains in quarantine.

We made friends.

We wrestled.

We played trains **and...**

we had fun in quarantine.

About the Author

LACEY J. HEINZ is a reading enthusiast. Her love of reading was cultivated by her mother at an early age. As a child, she dreamed of sharing her affinity for reading with other children and one day becoming an author. Now that dream is coming true. Lacey has a bachelor's degree in Elementary Education as well as a Reading Minor. In 2018, she received a master's in Education. Lacey lives in Puyallup, Washington, with her husband and two children, who were the inspiration for this story.

About the Illustrator

HANNAH MOORE has been drawing since she could hold a pencil, and learned how to paint from her mother who is a watercolor artist. Also an avid reader and storyteller, she began creating and illustrating her own stories for fun at a young age. Eventually, her love of books and art would lead her to major in both Graphic Design and Creative Writing. She lives in Seattle, Washington, where she is a Graphic Designer by day and an aspiring novelist by night.

Lacey and Hannah have wanted to work together on a children's book since they were in middle school. This project is a testament to their friendship and their dedication to achieving their goals.

CPSIA information can be obtained
at www.ICGtesting.com
Printed in the USA
LVHW021459121220
673925LV00005B/463

9 781480 894716